ALIEN MY POCKET

The Science Unfair

by
Nate Ball

illustrated by
Macky Pamintuan

HARPER
An Imprint of HarperCollinsPublishers

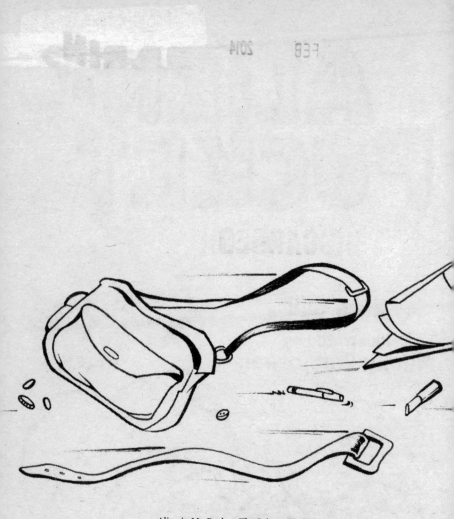

Alien in My Pocket: The Science UnFair

www.harpercollinschildrens.com
ISBN 978-0-06-221625-0
Typography by Sean Boggs

13 14 15 16 17 OPM 10 9 8 7 6 5 4 3 2 1
❖
First Edition

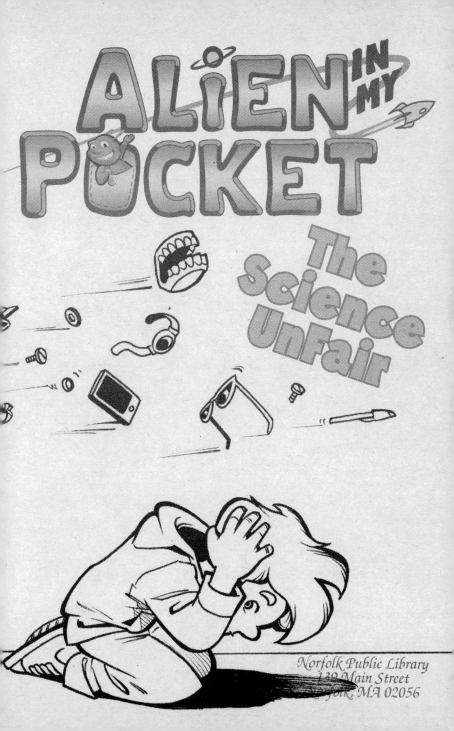

ALIEN IN MY POCKET

POCKET

The Science Unfair

Contents

01

Totally Crackers

I'm guessing you can't imagine how your life gets turned upside down when an alien flies through your bedroom window and crash-lands his spaceship on your bed.

I know I couldn't. Until it happened to me.

My life wasn't just turned upside down; it was pulled inside out, tied in a knot, and beaten like an egg.

At least that's what it felt like.

As I've learned, this alien was named Amp. He was from the planet Erde. He was sent to Earth to gather information about how to take over our planet. But after his first day here, he decided that attacking Earth would be a disaster for the people of Erde. Humans were too big—Amp was no bigger than a fat hamster—and too hard to predict.

Problem was, his ship wasn't working and his

radio wasn't transmitting. Amp had no way to call off the attack. We had more than a few days, but not more than a few months. So an impending attack on planet Earth by a bunch of Erdian dudes not much bigger than avocados was always in the back of our minds—though if the Erdian dudes are like Amp, I can't say I'm too worried.

"We need more Ritz crackers," Amp said, pulling on my lower lip.

"Amp, I'm sleeping," I mumbled, not opening my eyes. "Let go of my lip."

"All you do is sleep," he said, yanking my bottom lip up over my top lip. "Can you go down to the kitchen and get me some more?"

I opened one eye and focused it as best I could on my glowing clock. "It's 3:12 in the morning, Amp! I'm off duty."

At that point, my secret alien roommate released my lip and proceeded to dump Ritz cracker crumbs from the crinkly paper wrapper all over my face.

"AMP!" I shouted, sitting up, flicking crumbs from my eyelids, snorting crumbs out of my nose. "That was just rude," I hissed.

"Well, as long as you're up," his high-pitched

3

voice said from the dark, "you might as well go on a Ritz cracker run. I'll wait here."

It may sound cute and harmless and fascinating to have a four-inch-tall, blue-skinned, three-fingered alien hanging out in your room, but he was getting under my skin. My life as a fourth grader was slipping out of control.

Amp's diet of Ritz crackers and SweeTarts was also becoming annoying. He had no need for variety. Worst of all, he apparently never slept.

"Have you seen my helmet?" he asked.

"I can't see anything! It's dark!" I snapped. "Humans need to sleep, okay? We've gone over this, Amp. Now pipe down, or I'll drop-kick you all the way back to Erde." I collapsed back into my warm pillow.

My outburst won me just five seconds of silence. "Touchy," came his reply.

"Annoying," I said between clenched teeth.

I heard Amp whisper into the little device he wore on his wrist.

"Council Note: Humans appear to need to lie down, close their eyes,

4

and breathe deeply for eight hours a day. It appears necessary for them to function well and stay healthy."

"What I wouldn't give for eight hours," I growled. "You keep me up most nights."

"I'm unsure how this civilization ever gets things done," he concluded.

"I'm unsure why I haven't stuffed that voice recorder up your nose," I simmered.

"Do you mind if I turn on the lights?" he said.

AAGH! That was it! I slapped the mattress with both hands, threw my legs off the side of the bed, and yanked up my covers as I stood.

"WHOA!" came Amp's cry, as he was sent tumbling somewhere in the blackness. Served him right.

"You need to work on your manners," I growled. As I pulled open my door, I heard one of my little brother's crawling robots scamper past my feet and into my room. Reaching out quickly with my foot, I flipped it onto its back and into the hall. Its gears and legs worked furiously, trying to find the floor. Was everybody in this house trying to drive me insane?

Without another word, I stomped down the hall, descended the stairs, and did a face-plant on the living room couch. I was finally safe from Amp's pestering. He rarely left my room on account of Mr. Jinxy, our cat; Smokey, our dog; and Taylor, my pesky little brother.

Since Amp had entered my life, my grades had headed south, my parents thought I had con-centration issues, and my chances of making the travel baseball team were fading fast. Worst of all, my hope for the future of mankind was starting to dim.

All this, plus too many nights on our lumpy couch.

Lucky for me, before my eyes could start tear-ing up, I fell asleep.

As you can see, living with an alien is a lot harder than it sounds.

02

Couch Head

"**W**ow, it looks like your head is exploding," my little brother Taylor said when he saw my roosterlike hairdo. "Did you cock-a-doodle-doo at sunrise?"

I gave him a blank stare.

I was still in my pajamas, wrapped in my sheets and blankets. My eyes were only half open. I had managed to make it to the fridge before plopping down at the kitchen table, but hadn't yet made it upstairs to get ready for school.

Apparently, I had bedhead.

"Whoa, it's the ghost of Christmas past," my dad exclaimed, bursting into the kitchen and making a beeline to the coffee pot. "Is that what you're wearing to school?"

Everybody in my house was a comedian.

"Well, look what the cat dragged in," my mom

chuckled when she saw me half-asleep in front of my slice of cold pizza. She folded her arms and gave me the look. "How are things going with General Washington at Valley Forge?"

"Funny, Mom," I said, closing my eyes.

"Cold pizza?" she said with a *tsk-tsk*. She snatched the slice away before I could grab it. "Let me get something proper for a growing baseball player. I picked up thirteen SweeTart wrappers in your room yesterday."

I groaned. "Mom, please don't go snooping in my room."

"Since when is putting clean and folded laundry in your room snooping?" she said, digging around in the refrigerator.

"Zack slept on the couch again," Taylor tattletaled. "I thought he was a robber. I almost hit him in the head with a lamp."

"With that hairdo, it looks like you actually did," Dad said, not looking up from reading emails on his smartphone.

"And who were you talking to all night?" Taylor asked. "Do you have someone hiding in your room?"

I gulped.

"Oh dear, you've been talking in your sleep again?" Mom said, spooning peach yogurt into a small bowl.

"It's not just talking," Taylor continued. "It's like he's arguing and doing weird voices."

"I've also heard you up at odd hours of the night, dear. Maybe I should call Dr. Bell and ask him what he thinks." She placed the yogurt in front of me.

"I hate yogurt," I said flatly.

"You don't *hate* anything," Dad said, looking up from his phone. "You dislike things, Zack, you do not hate them."

"Oh, I dislike a lot of things," I said. "But yogurt I definitely hate."

"Fine, I'll make you eggs," Mom said, giving the bowl of yogurt to my dad.

"I dislike yogurt," Dad said, giving me a sideways glance and pushing the yogurt in front of my brother. Taylor happily attacked the bowl of peach yogurt with one of the electric spoons he had invented.

I honestly felt like crying.

"I've got an email here from your teacher, Miss Martin," Dad said slowly, apparently reading as he spoke.

"Uh-oh, that can't be good," Taylor said.

"She says everyone's ideas for the science fair are due today," he said.

"I'm doing a new spider robot," Taylor announced proudly.

"Son, this is your chance," Dad said, raising an eyebrow at me. "The science fair project is fifty percent of your science grade."

"What are you going to do, Zack?" my mom asked as she cracked eggs into a sizzling frying pan.

"It's kind of hard to explain," I lied.

"That means he doesn't have an idea yet," Taylor said.

Dad gave Taylor a look, then turned back to me. "You remember our deal: if your grades slip, no baseball."

I stared at the spot on the table where my cold pizza used to be. "I swear I'm all set with something really good," I lied. Again.

My mom turned around from the stove. "I'm

sure it'll be great, Zack. You started off with such a bang, but you've seemed a bit distracted lately. It sounds like you have your focus back now."

"It does?" Taylor squawked. "Look at him. He looks like he got run over by a tractor."

"That's enough," Dad said to Taylor.

Taylor made a face at me.

A steaming plate of gross-looking, half-cooked scrambled eggs was placed before me. It reminded me of my life: a steaming, gooey mess. "Ugh," I said.

I needed an idea for my science project fast, and I knew just who was going to help me come up with one.

03

Dumber and Dumbest

Amp sat on the alarm clock I kept next to my bed. My mom was waiting downstairs to drive me to school. The time on the clock told me I had missed the bus fifteen minutes ago and would probably be late for school.

"Listen, Amp, I have a D in science right now," I said with as much patience as I could muster. "Miss Martin told us—"

"What's the D stand for?" he interrupted.

"It stands for . . . ," I began, trying to remember what the D stood for. "I can't remember! The D stands for disaster, okay? Or dummy! Or dimwit! It doesn't matter what it stand for. It's bad!"

"If it stands for bad, it should be a B, not a D," he said.

"No, a B is good," I said.

"Good should be a G then, right?"

"Gosh dang it, Amp!" I howled. "You can't change the grading system that's been around since my parents were kids. You're missing the main point."

"Hey, I have a great idea for a science experiment."

"Oh, yeah. What?"

"I'd need some special equipment, of course, and I'd need to sequence a sample of your DNA, but growing a third arm would be really interesting, and easier than you think."

I stared at him. He was either clueless or intentionally trying to make me angry. I could never tell which. "I can't grow another arm!" I shouted. "None of my shirts would fit."

"But you'd be a heck of a juggler," he said softly.

"I can put you in a hamster cage, you know," I said.

"Okay," he said, holding up both hands in surrender. "I'm just asking that you think about it."

I grabbed my head and squeezed it, which, surprisingly, helped me remember something. I jumped up and pulled my science textbook out of my backpack and flipped through the pages. There were twenty or so suggestions for classroom experiments in the glossary in the back. One caught my eye. It showed a potato with a bunch of wires stuck in it and a small lightbulb that was lit up next to it. It was labeled POTATO BATTERY. All I'd need was a potato, some wires, and a lightbulb. How hard could that be?

"Easy," I announced. "I'm going to make a battery out of a potato."

I dropped the book on my bed and pointed to the two photos.

Amp leaped onto the bed and stepped onto the open page. He read in silence. Studied the photos for a minute, stroking his tiny blue chin the whole time.

"Seems kind of dull," he said.

"No, it seems easy. A simple potato battery is perfect."

"Whoa, someone didn't brush his teeth this morning," Amp said, waving his hand in front of his face.

"Funny," I said. "That's what I'm making."

"Fine, but I should warn you that—"

Just then my door popped open and my mom stuck her head in.

I whipped my head in Amp's direction.

But Amp was gone. I looked around, but, thankfully, he had vanished. Mom hadn't noticed. He really was the fastest thing I had ever seen— or not seen.

"Who on earth are you talking to up here?"

"I'm . . . I'm practicing my science fair presentation," I said weakly.

"You're still doing your homework, Zack?" She sighed. "C'mon, I need to get to work. Better fix that hair first, honey." She headed back down the hallway.

"One second, Mom," I called after her.

"Between her popping in all the time and your brother snooping around, I'm getting nervous about being discovered."

I froze. "What? Taylor's been in here? Looking around? Has he seen you?"

"No, because I usually make myself invisible. Would you like me to tell you how?"

"No, I don't care how. We just can't get caught.

If someone sees you they'll take you away, Amp. Then you'll never get home."

Amp looked concerned. "One of these days our luck will run out, Zack. I think your brother is suspicious. We need to get my spaceship repaired!"

"We will, Amp. As soon as I get through this science fair. I can only handle one disaster at a time."

04

Potato Power

"I'm going to make a battery out of a potato," I said quietly to Miss Martin.

I was standing next to her desk. The classroom was silent. They were all staring at me. I was like a car wreck on the interstate. You might have wanted to look away, but you just couldn't.

Miss Martin looked up from the science fair binder spread out in front of her. She was writing down each student's science project idea next to their name. "And do you have the registration form signed by your parents?"

My stomach dropped like a broken elevator. "Uh, I forgot about the form," I said as quietly as I could.

Miss Martin stared at me with disappointment. I squirmed.

"Zack, you need to bring that form tomorrow."

"Consider it done," I said and smiled.

"So does your science fair project test a hypothesis?" I looked at her blankly. "What do you hope to prove with your experiment?" she asked patiently, waiting to write down my response in her notebook.

I gulped. "I just hope to prove that I can do it," I said.

"Do what?" she asked.

"Do the project, of course," I said with a shrug.

"That doesn't sound like a hypothesis," she said.

"Oh, the *high*-pothesis," I said as if I'd misheard her the first time. I proceeded to nod my head for twenty seconds, trying to think of something to say. "I am going to prove that yams work better than potatoes. You know, when it comes to using vegetables for batteries."

Miss Martin stared at me dead-on for a full ten seconds. "Yams vs. potatoes," she said coldly. "Okay, please return to your desk and see to it that you bring me that signed form tomorrow, Zackary Frederick McGee."

"That should not be a problem," I said.

I returned to my desk, sank into my seat, and

opened my science workbook to our assignment. "I hate science crossword puzzles," I said louder than I should have.

"You don't hate crossword puzzles," a familiar voice said. "You dislike them."

Olivia.

Olivia was my best friend and next-door neighbor. We spend a lot of time together. She's also the only other person on this planet who knows about Amp.

"What's your project?" she whispered.

"I'm doing a potato battery. Potatoes can generate, you know, electricity."

"Really?" she whispered. "Sounds pretty boring."

"Ugh," I groaned, letting my head drop to my desk.

"What's with your hair today?" she asked. "It looks like you're wearing a crown back here." She started mashing down my hair.

I jerked away. "Why is everybody so obsessed with my hair?"

"Touchy," she whispered in my ear.

"I should have just worn a hat," I grumbled.

"Are you done building your experiment?" she asked, poking my shoulder.

23

I sank a little in my chair. "I haven't started yet."

"You better get on it, rooster head."

"I know, I know," I mumbled as my eyes started to close.

"What's wrong with you?" she asked with real concern in her voice. "Did you eat breakfast? It's the most important meal of the day, you know."

But I didn't answer. I had fallen asleep. A sweet, deep, and extra-sudden sleep. I dreamed of dancing yams and potatoes. Soon, they began to fight with tiny toothpick swords. The battlefield became a huge potato salad of fallen spuds. It was the kind of dream that makes you hungry for a picnic.

I slept in my chair for a good ten minutes and nobody noticed. When the bell for recess finally rang, I jumped three feet in the air and everybody laughed.

I was becoming the class goofball, and my bad hair wasn't the only reason.

And now I was counting on a yam and a potato to save my bacon.

Seemed unlikely.

05

Spy Games

When I got home that afternoon, I just wanted to take a nap. I zombie-walked through the kitchen, stumbled up the stairs, and did a soaring swan dive onto my bed.

"OUCH!" my bed said.

I sat up and froze. "Amp?"

"You almost killed me!" my bed said again.

I gasped. "Amp? Are you hurt?" I cried. I leaped off my bed and started gently shaking my blankets. "Amp?" I called desperately. "Did I flatten you, buddy? You've got to be more careful. . . ."

"Who's Amp?" my bed asked.

"What the—," I yelped. I dropped to my knees and looked under my bed. I came face-to-face with my little brother, Taylor. "WHY, YOU LITTLE SPY!"

"Mom, help!" he screeched as I yanked him

out from under the bed by his leg. "Zack is going to kill me!"

I sat on his chest and grabbed him roughly by the collar of his T-shirt. "You're not allowed to be in here!"

"Who's Amp?" he asked in a bratty voice.

"None of your business," I said.

"Does he own that spaceship in your closet?"

"Spaceship?"

"I'm gonna tell Mom and Dad. You've got a UFO."

It took me a moment. My brain spun. Then it hit me: Taylor had found Amp's spaceship under the blanket in my closet. "It's not what you think it is."

"Is it Amp's?"

"You know what it is?" I growled.

"What?" he said, staring up at me with a dumb smirk.

"None of your business." I pulled him up, opened my door, pushed him into the hallway, and slammed the door. "STAY OUTTA MY ROOM!"

"I'm telling Mom," he shouted from the other side of the door. I could hear him run off.

"That was close," Amp said. He appeared standing on my desk, looking worried. "He almost saw me."

"We have to hide your spaceship better. Right now," I stammered. "Can you make it disappear? I need some serious Erdian hocus-pocus, like pronto."

"I'm an alien, not a magician, Zack! I can't make inanimate things disappear."

I ran into my closet, lifted up his spaceship, carried it to my hamper, and dumped it in.

Then I crawled around on my floor, snatched up some dirty clothes, and threw them into the hamper, covering up the spaceship.

"Oh, that's nice," he growled at me. "An advanced space- and time-bending spacecraft covered with your stinky socks and underpants."

I heard them coming.

I raced to my closet and searched my shelves frantically. Then I saw something that was perfect.

By the time Taylor arrived, pulling Mom by the hand through my room, I was pretending to relax on my bed.

"He's got it hidden under this blanket," I heard

Taylor say from inside my closet. There was a moment of silence. "Huh? That wasn't here before!" he said, confused. "He must have moved it, Mom, I swear."

"That's just Zack's old hamster cage," Mom said sternly. "Enough with this nonsense—and stay out of your brother's room."

I watched cheerfully as Mom marched my little brother past my bed and out the door. She was holding him by the earlobe in a pinch that looked like it must have hurt.

"Have a nice day," I said gleefully, jumping up and gently closing my door.

"I need to fix my ship and leave this place as soon as I can," Amp said from behind me. "If word gets out you're hiding an alien in your room, I'll never escape. They'll take my ship apart. Maybe me, too. They'll do tests on me. I may not look it, but really I'm very delicate."

"I promise, Amp, you'll get my full attention after Wednesday's science fair."

06

Slapdash Science

The next day, Miss Martin was unimpressed with the paperwork for my experiment. "Did you write this on the school bus?" she asked without looking up.

That was definitely not a compliment. I remained silent.

After giving it the once-over and a few *tsk-tsk* sounds, she pulled a tiny lightbulb out of the cabinet behind her desk. "If your potato can make this flashlight bulb glow, it will make for a more interesting experiment."

"Don't forget about the yam," I said.

"Oh, how could I?" she said flatly. "This bulb will require at least 1.5 volts and roughly 10 milliamps of current to make it light up," she said slowly, dropping it into an envelope and handing it to me.

"That sounds about right," I said, clearly not knowing what I was saying.

I slunk back to my desk. Everyone around me was buzzing with excitement about their crummy science experiments. Everyone but me, that is. In fact, it sounded like everybody had already finished building their experiments. I hadn't even started mine.

Davey Swope was building a volcano that spit out spaghetti sauce. Nino Sasso was hatching flies in big jars, but nobody was sure why. Max Myers had a machine that could measure the strength of a head-butt on a giant digital scoreboard. Me? I had some vegetables and a light the size of my pinky nail.

Just when I thought it couldn't get any worse, the science really hit the fan. Miss Martin stood up and announced that we needed to demonstrate our experiments in front of the class on Monday, a full two days before the Reed School Science Fair Competition.

"There goes my weekend," I groaned.

So on Friday after school, instead of playing baseball up at the park, riding my bike to 7-Eleven for a

Slurpee, or watching a scary movie with Olivia, I had to gather materials to build my lousy experiment.

And it required a ton of stuff.

The potato was easy; I took one from our kitchen. The yam I had to borrow from Olivia's grandfather. For some reason, he made me promise to give it back after I was done with it. And for the rest, my mom had to drive me to the hardware store. She made me pay for it all out of my allowance, too.

By the time we were done running errands, I just wanted to finish my experiment as fast as possible. Tryouts for this fall's travel baseball team were Saturday afternoon. I was sure no catcher in the history of baseball had ever effectively blocked wild pitches while they were thinking about yams, potatoes, wires, and flashlight bulbs.

I decided to build my experiment at my dad's worktable in the garage. With my science book for guidance, I managed to whip the whole thing together in about twenty minutes. That includes time for labeling for the project, which I wrote directly onto the cardboard with a Sharpie to save paper.

Done and done.

I left my science project behind and went inside to beg for pizza. I really didn't think I'd have to spend another minute on my science project the entire weekend.

Boy, was I wrong.

Scientific Train Wreck

"No offense, Zack, but it looks like you made this while blindfolded and riding a unicycle. And tell me again: what's the pillowcase for?"

Olivia had uncovered my experiment, which I'd cloaked in one of Taylor's Star Wars pillowcases. She'd been staring at it for a good five minutes already.

"Presentation," I sighed. "It's all in the presentation. Besides, it works. Look at the bulb. That's all that matters."

Olivia cupped her hands around the tiny bulb and focused a squinted eye about an inch from it. "Barely," she said, unimpressed.

"I never imagined you'd need to tape the potato and yam down with so much duct tape," Amp said quietly, looking at my project like it was science roadkill.

"Oh, no," Olivia mumbled.

"What?" I said, trying not to care about the feedback I was getting.

"You spelled potato with an e on the end," Olivia said, looking at my project's label. "And the word 'battery' has two t's, not one." She shook her head. "You've got two spelling errors, and that's just in the title."

"Are you sure? Those look right to me," I said. "Besides, it's a science fair, not a spelling bee, Olivia."

"Without a meter, how can you accurately demonstrate that one vegetable is producing more electricity than the other?" Amp asked, stroking his chin with concern.

"Would you two just stop?" I snapped. "It's fine. I don't need to win the Prentice Science Scholarship, I just need an A."

"An A?" Olivia yelped. "Zack, you'll be lucky if you don't get detention when you bring this in on Monday."

"Why me?" I groaned. I flopped onto my bed and covered my face with my baseball glove. "I'm just not scientifically oriented. It's like a disability. You can't hold that against me."

"On the bright side, you do have a knack for sloppiness," Amp said, barely holding back a laugh. "So you are indeed gifted in certain ways."

"The two of you are giving me a headache," I moaned.

The room got quiet. I could practically hear them staring at my project. I knew what they were saying was true. My project was terrible. Everybody would laugh at me. A blanket of doom settled over me. For a moment, I considered running away from home and joining the Navy.

I felt Olivia sit heavily on the corner of my bed. She sighed. "Zacky, you know me. I'm a fixer. I'm here to help," Olivia said quietly.

I sat up and the glove fell from my face. "Really? Then let's fix it pronto, so we can go watch a zombie movie."

"I'm afraid I think it needs more than a quick fix. I think we should start over," Amp declared.

I groaned in protest. "Start over? Completely?"

"Oh, yes," Amp said. He cleared his throat. "This electric yam experiment is really beneath someone as clever as you, Zack."

"But Zack already turned in his paperwork," Olivia said.

"I saw that paperwork. It was terrible. Your teacher will be thrilled if you redo it."

"Redo it?" I protested. "Seriously, guys, I don't have time for this," I complained.

"Yes, that's why we're going to save you from yourself," Olivia said.

"So," Amp declared with a wave of his arm, "let's show everyone at Reed School that Zack McGee has an enthusiasm for science that burns a whole lot brighter than a tiny light attached to a sad-looking potato."

"Let's do it," Olivia said, jumping up and shaking me by the shoulders. "Let's rock that science fair with some wickedly cool science, Zacky Boy!"

"Okay, okay," I said, my head wobbling from Olivia's shaking. I looked over at Amp. "So what are we going to build?"

"I have no idea," Amp said.

"Oh, brother," I said and flopped back onto my bed.

"Don't you worry, Dr. Frankenstein," Olivia said, patting me on the knee. "We'll think of something."

08

The Big Idea

Olivia and I didn't say much as Amp carefully studied each of the experiments in the glossary at the back of my science textbook.

"Interesting," Amp said in his peculiar high-pitched voice.

"What?" I said. "Is it something we can build fast?"

"Maybe not as fast as you'd like, but it certainly could be spectacular."

"Really?" Olivia said, looking up from the doodle she'd been making on a piece of binder paper. "Spectacular sounds like just what we're looking for."

"We're going to build an electromagnet," Amp announced.

My shoulders slumped. "That's it? Sounds boring."

Amp was whispering into his recorder:

**"Council Note concerning the
Earthlings—"**

"Who is he talking to?" Olivia asked me.

"See? He does that all the time! It's like his tape recorder. It makes me nuts."

**"Earthlings have discovered they
can create a magnetic field with
coiled wire and electricity. But they
seem not to know that the amount
of magnetism they create this way is
tiny. They don't appear to realize that
magnetism is one of the most useful
forces in all of nature. More later."**

"Hey, blue boy," Olivia said, snapping her fingers in exasperation. "I agree with Zack. Sounds kinda ho-hum."

Amp remained calm. "I'm not suggesting we build this exact experiment. Why would we? I'm saying we do it the right way."

"You're saying we supersize it?" Olivia said, clapping with excitement.

"Exactly," Amp said. "By building a large enough coil and sending extremely high levels of current through the wire in repeated, short bursts, we'll tear the belt buckle right off of Mr. Luntz!"

Olivia laughed and got up and whooped around the room.

I was not convinced. "What about all my work on the potato thing?"

Olivia laughed. "You have to ace this, Zack! And what better way than with a little spaceman hocus-pocus?"

"BUT I'VE GOT BASEBALL TRYOUTS THIS AFTERNOON!" I shouted, and then fell onto my bed like a guy falling backward into a swimming pool.

The room got quiet. My secret was out. The truth was I just wanted to focus on baseball, not science or yams or wires or electromagnets.

I was trying out for catcher, but I hadn't caught a pitch with my catcher's mitt since Amp arrived. This was my chance to make the fall travel team, and I really didn't want something stupid like homework to mess it up.

Amp shook his tiny head. "Are you telling me baseball is more important to you than science?"

"Of course!" I shouted, staring at the ceiling. "I know Erdians don't do anything but invade other planets, but on Earth, we have, like, games. And they're, like, fun."

"Well, all I know is that if you turn that in," Olivia said, poking my sad-looking potato- and yam-battery experiment, "you can kiss baseball good-bye."

"Uuuuugh," I groaned. I wanted to cry. I wanted to toss my stupid experiment out the window. I felt trapped. I felt cornered. I felt like eating a giant plate of nachos, for some reason.

"Okay," I said quietly. "We can build this electric magnet thingy, but this is the only weekend of try-outs for new players. And I am so not missing it."

"How about we work on the experiment while you're out playing baseball?" Olivia offered.

"You'd do that for me?" I said, feeling genuinely touched.

"We know how important this is to you," Olivia said, reaching out to put an arm around Amp but settling instead for just a finger.

45

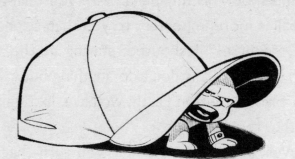

"Actually, Olivia, the baseball thing is a mystery to me," Amp said. "Seems like a colossal waste of time hitting a ball with a stick and running around in circles."

"Shush," Olivia said, dropping one of my baseball hats over Amp.

"Hey!" he shouted from inside the hat

"I can't believe I have to make two experiments in one weekend," I said, burying my face in my pillow. "It's like science prison."

"Once you see this experiment," Amp said, crawling out from under my hat, "you won't even remember that yam of yours. Now, first things first. I'll need some SweeTarts and Ritz crackers."

"Oh, good grief," I croaked. "What have I gotten myself into?"

09

Bolts and Zucchinis

Watching Amp eat a Ritz cracker was maddening. He held each cracker—which was probably twice the size of his head—with both hands and turned it in a quick circle, nibbling the edge as it went around. Cracker crumbs went everywhere, until it vanished. Then Amp licked each of his six fingers.

It was like watching a squirrel who'd had too much coffee.

Watching him eat SweetTarts was even worse. He flicked each one into the air, caught it in his mouth, and swallowed it whole.

"So let's get to it," I said. I went to my closet, grabbed my catcher's mitt off the shelf, and pulled it on. "I gotta leave in two hours. What's first?"

Amp scratched his head and nodded, thinking. "We need a huge nail or metal rod. Thick. Preferably iron."

"Why iron?" Olivia asked.

Amp looked at us in disbelief. He turned his back and spoke into the recorder on his wrist.

"Council Note: Earth's plentiful supply of iron is something to consider. Iron is an element whose atoms form magnetic domains that are aligned extremely easily by an outside magnetic field. The huge amplification of the field that results means it's a perfect material for building an electromagnet. This

element would be useful back on Erde. Further study required."

"Amp, it's kinda creepy when you do that, you know?" Olivia said.

"Yeah," I agreed. "You realize we can totally hear you, right?"

"Consider it a lovable quirk of mine," he said.

Olivia picked up my textbook and stared closely at the photo of our experiment. "Looks like they just use a regular old steel nail in the book, Amp."

"Hey, my dad has a huge bolt," I said, remembering a gift the school board gave him for getting the city to install a streetlight at the corner near my school. "It's one of those big fat ones that hold up those streetlight poles. It's bigger than a zucchini."

"Great!" Amp exclaimed. "Quick, go get it. Pure iron would be best, but even if it's steel, it might do what we need if it's big enough. We're not just going to build any old electromagnet."

I paused. "Oh, I can't," I said. "Not now."

"Why not?" Olivia said, throwing up her arms.

"It's in his office, and he's in there. It's sort of mounted on this trophy thing."

49

"Then we can't use it," Olivia said.

"I just need to swipe it when he's not around. He won't miss it. Plus, we can return it when we're done, right?"

We both looked at Amp. He shrugged. "Sure, I don't see why not. We're also going to need wire. Thick wire. It has to have insulation on it, like a plastic or rubber casing. And we need a lot: enough to wrap tightly around your zucchini-bolt a lot of times."

We all sat in silence, thinking.

I pulled one of the wires off the yam on my experiment. "Could we use this?"

"Totally unacceptable," Amp said. "Too short. Too thin."

Olivia jumped up. "Hey, if you kept the receipt you could return these wires and buy the kind we need."

I sighed. "I'm sure my mom has it. She keeps the receipt for everything. But I'd have to explain to her that I've changed my experiment. Plus, I'd have to go to back to the hardware store. No experiment is worth that."

"Too bad," Olivia said. She started stuffing my experiment's wires back into the plastic bag they had come in. "We can swing by the hardware store before we drop you off at tryouts."

"We?" I said.

Olivia patted my shoulder. "I'll tell your mom you've gotten excited about science again. Let your pal Olivia handle the details."

"Oh, this is turning into a total nightmare," I said, holding the mitt to my face.

"Amp and I will keep working while you're playing catch and hitting your balls."

I couldn't even respond to that one.

With a growl, I grabbed the bag with all my baseball gear. My weekend had been hijacked. I was no longer in charge of my own science experiment. And making the baseball team suddenly seemed like a long shot.

Worst of all, I just wanted to take a nap.

Sleep Magnet

"**I** asked you if you realized that the Earth itself is one big magnet," Amp said.

"What? What time is it?"

"Don't worry about the time. Worry about what I'm telling you," Amp's voice needled from somewhere in the dark.

I groaned and peered at the glowing numbers on my alarm clock with one half-closed eye. 2:46 a.m.

I couldn't see Amp, or I would have backhanded him off my bed and through the wall.

"What is Earth's core made out of?" Amp's voice asked casually.

"Oh, c'mon, I don't know," I moaned.

"Think about it."

"Sugar and spice and everything nice?"

"That is a horrible guess," he said.

Then I heard him whispering into his ridiculous recorder.

**"Council Note: Human children
seem unaware that their planet
is primarily made out of iron. And
that some of it is molten, which,
of course, means it's in a heated,
liquid state. All of which helps
make this planet one big magnet.
Not only do they not know, they
don't even seem to care, which
may explain their failure to achieve
interplanetary travel. Amp over."**

"Stop talking into your arm, please," I said, closing my eyes. "And we have been to the moon, wise guy."

"Oh dear, the moon is not a planet," Amp sighed. "It's a . . . well, it's a moon."

I didn't care. I was exhausted. Baseball tryouts had sapped whatever interest I had in my lousy experiment. Plus, my neck hurt like crazy.

The tryouts had actually gone better than

I imagined they would. I hit the ball better than ever. But toward the end of the session, I had to catch pitches thrown by Max Myers, a fellow fourth grader who looked like a truck driver with anger issues.

Max didn't so much pitch as catapult the ball in my direction with a whirling and wild windmill motion. He was all speed and no control. Not only did his fastballs make my hand feel like it was melting inside my mitt, many of them bounced before the plate.

Toward the end, one of Max's wild pitches caught the front edge of home plate, ricocheted off my glove, and shot straight up under my mask and off the side of my neck.

Catchers are never supposed to let a pitch get past them, no matter how badly it's thrown. The catcher's curse, my dad called it. All three coaches were watching. But I kept Max's wild pitch in front of me. That's what matters. I could tell the coaches were impressed by the way they didn't stop spitting sunflower seeds.

I started dozing off again thinking about it, but Amp was on a roll.

"See, Earth itself is one big magnet," he declared. "It has two poles, just like a magnet. The Earth's magnetic moment is really huge, meaning its ability to exert magnetic force on things is super big."

"I'm having a moment of my own right now," I

said. "A moment of pain."

Amp ignored me. "I think I've found a way to provide a boost to our little experiment. My ship has a small device that can tap into a bit of Earth's magnetic field," Amp said. "Does adding that sound okay?"

"Nothing anybody says at three in the morning sounds okay," I said, keeping my eyes closed. "Even Mrs. Einstein told Albert to shut up at three in the morning."

"Splendid," he said. I could hear him clapping, which sounded like two marshmallows being thumped together. "I'll get to work right away."

"Terrific," I said, mostly into my pillow.

Looking back, I wish I had paid closer attention to what he was saying. Only later would I realize the mistake I had just made.

11

Breakfast Breakdown

I stood frozen in the kitchen doorway early the next morning.

"It's about time, Rip Van Winkle," Olivia said.

She was sitting cheerfully with my family at our kitchen table.

"What are you doing here?" I blurted out, looking down at the pajamas I was wearing, the ones I had outgrown two years ago. "I'm not even dressed."

"Oh, hush up," Mom said. "She's here to help with your project. A girl can't do science on an empty stomach." She smiled at Olivia.

My mom loved Olivia. She was the daughter Mom never had.

"Olivia's been telling us all about your new science project," Dad said, looking up from his smartphone.

"She has?" I croaked.

That's the thing about Olivia. She loves to talk. And half the things she says make me cringe. I constantly worry that she'll spill the beans about Amp by accident one day. She talks so fast and says so much it seems bound to happen.

"She thinks your new experiment could go all the way to the tri-county finals this year," said Taylor, looking up from his oozing egg yolk. "Gosh, you should have worn a robe or something, Zack."

"Why should I have to wear a robe in my own house?" I complained.

"Where else would you wear a robe, except in your own house?" Dad asked, without looking up from an email he was reading.

I skittered to the last open chair and sat quickly, covering myself as best I could with a napkin.

Taylor looked at Olivia suspiciously. "She thinks it's even better than my robot last year."

Taylor was not only the first kid in kindergarten to enter our school's science fair, he won it. He had built a robot that flipped pancakes. The robot's name was Flip. Get it? Anyway, he was out to prove that a robot could cook a pancake better than a person. He called his experiment "The Big Flip-Off!"

Taylor had some parents who came to the science fair face off against the robot over a big, two-foot griddle. When Taylor and Flip won first place, they both went to the Tri-County Science Fair Competition, where Taylor and his flapjack-flipping robot took second place. He was interviewed on the evening news. My mom posted a link to the interview on her Facebook page and got over three hundred likes.

"So, Zack, do you really think your magnet can top Flip?" Mom asked excitedly.

I groaned. "It's an electromagnet, and no, I'm just hoping to get an A. That's it."

"Really?" Dad said. "Olivia here says you're going for something truly spectacular."

I glared at Olivia. "Maybe she set the bar too high."

"I'm pretty sure my spider is gonna beat his lame-o magnet, Dad," Taylor boasted. "It actually weaves its own web."

"Really? Cool!" Olivia exclaimed. "Oh, that

sounds a lot better than Zack's magnet thingy."

I glared at her again. Olivia returned my glare with a fake smile and shoved a giant piece of bacon in her mouth.

"Is there any more bacon?" I asked, looking at the empty plate in the middle of the table.

"The early bird gets the bacon," Mom said, and laughed too hard at her own joke.

"Thanks," I sighed. "And don't forget, today is the second day of baseball tryouts." Nobody at the table seemed interested in my hopes and dreams. I cleared my throat. "If it's okay, I'm going to go change into something more comfortable."

"You mean something more uncomfortable," Taylor said.

I didn't answer. I zipped out of the kitchen, down the hallway, and into my dad's office. I walked over to the giant bolt that was resting on two wooden hooks that extended from a plaque mounted on the wall behind the desk. I lifted the bolt off the hooks. It was surprisingly heavy. I almost dropped it on my naked toes.

I tiptoed up the stairs holding the heavy bolt with both hands.

At the top step I froze. My ears had picked up on something faint.

High-pitched screaming.

Very high-pitched!

AMP! AMP WAS IN TROUBLE!

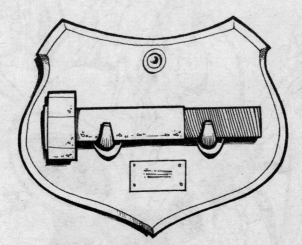

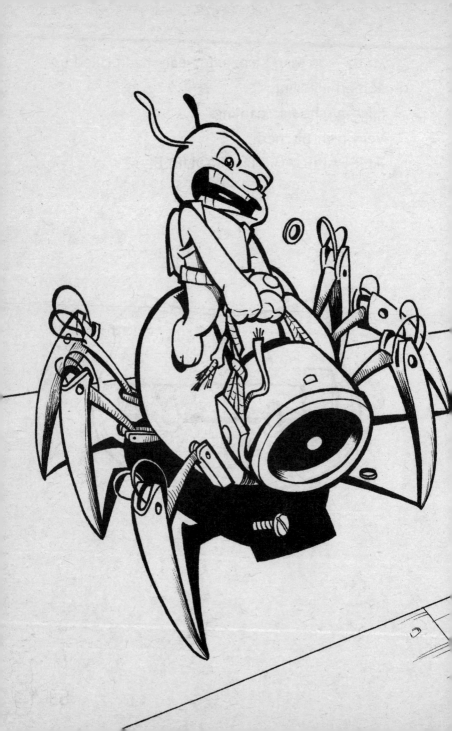

12

Spider Attack!

Still holding the doorknob, it took me a moment to understand what I was looking at.

Spider robots were crawling all over my bedroom floor. Each had a tiny video camera mounted on top of its body. They were scampering this way and that. One was under my bed. Its camera had become stuck on the edge of a blanket that hung down.

"Don't just stand there, Zack!" Amp squeaked. "HELP ME!"

I closed the door quickly, silently. "Where are you?"

"On the spider by the hamper!" he screeched in his squeaky voice.

Then I saw him clinging to the back of a frantic yellow spider.

The spider robot was rotating crazily around

and around in circles, then suddenly reversing direction, like it was trying to buck Amp. Amp was holding on for dear life. He had his hands on the wire leading to the back of the camera. With one great pull, he yanked out the wire and the camera's red light instantly went off. "These floofy things came out of nowhere! They have cameras."

"I can see that," I said.

"I can't be invisible to cameras," he growled, holding on to the tiny camera to keep from getting thrown. "I can only be invisible to a human being!"

"I thought you were kidding about the invisibility thing," I said.

"I'm getting captured on video right now. Look at these antennas. The video is being transmitted somewhere."

That shook me out of my frozen state.

I ran to my window, threw it open, flicked out the screen, and let it drop down into the bushes below in the backyard. Then I spun and, grabbing two robots at a time, flung them out my second-floor window. There were at least a dozen of them in different shapes and sizes. One was so small and so fast it took me half a minute just to catch it.

Soon they were all gone and the room was quiet. I peered down at them from my second-story window, trying to catch my breath. Some of the robots had exploded into pieces when they hit the patio. A few were upside down, moving their legs madly in the air. But half of them were still crawling, limping with their cameras across our backyard.

"What are you waiting for?" Amp cried.

I turned from the window and saw Amp at the door. "What now?" I cried.

"We have to erase whatever your brother's robots recorded!"

"Oh, right," I said. I scooped up Amp, emerged silently from my room, and crept quickly down the hall to my brother's room, being careful to avoid the hallway's squeaky spots. Everyone was still at the breakfast table, chatting away. I opened Taylor's door and stepped into what looked more like a robot factory than a kid's room.

"He must have been sending the signals back

to a recording device in his room," Amp said, leaping into action.

After some frenzied searching, we found a small antenna connected to a metal box near Taylor's laptop computer.

"This must be it," Amp instructed as I put him down on the computer. He popped opened the CD drive and somehow managed to crawl inside. I heard some banging and some strange sounding Erdian curse words. A few minutes later, he reemerged, dusty but no worse for wear. "That should take care of it," he said, smiling.

"You didn't just wreck his computer, did you?"

"Wreck it? No," Amp said. "But I wouldn't do any of your homework on it ever again."

13

Down to Business

As I came back downstairs, Taylor was blubbering like a baby. He had spotted his precious robots in pieces in the backyard. "Robot bully," he cried, pointing at me.

"Spy," I yelped right back.

Dad wasn't having any of it. He sent us both to our rooms. Olivia followed me upstairs. Amp was in his usual hiding place. We sat quietly until Olivia remembered the magnet wire we'd bought yesterday. That shook Amp from his glum mood. "This is perfect," he said, crawling out from the bookshelves to examine the wire. Olivia and I wrapped the wire around the giant bolt. "Leave no space between the wire, no overlapping," Amp pestered us. He made us start over again three times because he said it looked sloppy and uneven. The fourth time, we finally satisfied him.

"The more wraps around the bolt, the more grabbing power the electromagnet will have."

"It's a monster," Olivia exclaimed, admiring our handiwork.

I noticed about ten inches of wire hanging off each side of the bolt. "Should we cut this part off?"

"Heavens, no!" Amp cried. "That's where we attach it to the power source."

We used a bit of sandpaper to rub the coating off at both ends of the wire and attached them to a battery I took out of my flashlight. We were amazed at how easily the electromagnet picked up paper clips and tacks off my desk.

"Whoa!" Olivia and I exclaimed, amazed by its strength.

The instant a wire stopped making contact with the battery, the paper clips dropped to the desk.

"I thought it would make a noise," I said. "Like crackling electricity."

Amp shook his head at me. "Magnetism is generally silent," he said with a sigh.

"Pretty cool, Amp, but how do we make it

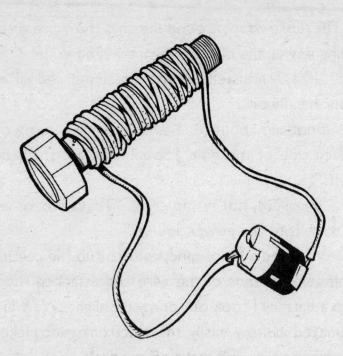

super-duper?" Olivia asked.

"It's all about the power source," he said. "Take my ship out of Zack's stinky hamper and I'll remove the battery from my ship. It's quite powerful."

"What if you win the whole enchilada?" Olivia asked me dreamily. "The winner gets to be on TV and their school gets five thousand bucks."

"Ah, who cares about that?" I said. "I just need to get my A and get on with my life."

After I removed Amp's ship from my hamper, he went to work somewhere inside of it. "Don't just stand there, start the paperwork," he shouted from inside the ship. "I plan on winning all the bananas on this one!"

Olivia and I looked at each other and laughed silently at Amp's bossiness. "What does 'winning all the bananas' even mean?" Olivia giggled.

I opened up my laptop to start on the paperwork that Miss Martin loved so much. Olivia was at my side the whole time. We even made a label for my project and spelled everything correctly.

By the time I had to go to baseball tryouts, everything seemed to have worked out perfectly. And my new science project was looking pretty spiffy.

"Should we test it more?" I asked.

"Go, go," Olivia said, pushing me in the back. "Amp and I will finish up and you'll be ready for your demonstration tomorrow."

I smiled. "This science stuff isn't so bad after all."

73

14

Magnetized

At dinner Monday night, I was puffed up with pride.

My in-class science project demonstration went off without a hitch. And even better, the three projects presented before mine were big duds. Davey Swope's volcano didn't erupt with spaghetti sauce, it just made a bad, burning-meatball smell. Max Myers head-butted his experiment so hard he disconnected the glowing display board and wound up in the nurse's office. And all of Nino Sasso's flies had died in their jars. He had to settle for explaining what should have happened if they had lived.

Then it was my turn.

As I stood nervously at the front of the class, everyone in front of me had seemed bored by my electromagnet. I hit the first button and a couple of paper clips jumped up and skittered across

Miss Martin's desk. Cool, but not enough to open anyone's eyes. Then I hit the second button.

Miss Martin's coffee cup of paper clips tipped over and about a hundred paper clips flew to the magnet like an angry swarm of bees to a jelly sandwich at a picnic lunch. A lizard-shaped metal paperweight shot across the room. An antique globe on a metal stand nearly broke my wrist as it careened across Miss Martin's desk.

All three objects seemed as if they were glued to my experiment. *CRACK! SLAP! SLAP!*

The entire class gasped.

It had all happened in the blink of an eye.

I slapped the power button off before it could do any serious damage. The metal objects fell to the desk with an audible *clunk*.

My classmates were utterly silent for a split second before exploding into applause. Even Max Myers gave me a standing hoot and fist-pump.

Whoa. A new science star was born.

After I told my family all the glorious details over beans and weenies—my mom's embarrassing name for pinto beans and hot dogs—Taylor said he had something to talk about, too.

"Look at these photos one of my robots took in Zack's room," he said, pretending to sound concerned. "I was able to save them off my hard drive."

"What?" I croaked.

"Not again, Taylor," Mom said.

As Taylor handed two photos to Dad, I snatched the other two from his other hand.

The photos weren't very clear, like those blurry pictures of Bigfoot running through the forest. But this Bigfoot was blue. One photo showed a fuzzy picture of Amp's tiny blue butt. The other was a close up of Amp's watery eye.

I did a big, fake, cackling laugh. "Oh, Taylor," I guffawed, "that's just one of Olivia's toys. It's a little elf doll she calls Amp." I handed the two photos to my mom, like I wasn't interested in them anymore.

I could feel Taylor staring at me.

"See, Taylor," Mom said with a *tsk-tsk*, "it's one of Olivia's toys. I think I've seen this toy in your room before, Zack."

"Oh, I'm sure you have," I said as steadily as I could.

"Looks almost real," Dad mumbled. He took

the two photos from Mom and stared at the close-up of Amp's eye. "Kind of creepy," he said.

"Oh, you have no idea how creepy and annoying that toy is," I said.

Taylor stood up slowly, his chair making a loud screeching noise on the tile floor. He stared at me, lips trembling, eyes blinking with anger.

He walked slowly out of the kitchen.

"What a weirdo," I said to Mom with an uneasy smile.

She sighed. "He's just upset," she said.

"He's not used to sharing the limelight," Dad agreed, shoveling in a spoonful of beans while staring at the photo of Amp's rear end.

"Well, he'll probably win tomorrow's science fair anyway," I said, trying to sound like the concerned older brother. "He'll get over it soon, I'm sure."

15

Showtime

Wednesday's science fair arrived without any further drama.

My experiment was bolted to a table next to Davey Swope's volcano and across from Max Myers's head-butting meter. At the time, I wasn't sure why Amp insisted on securing it to something heavy, but at that point I was more interested in watching Davey and Max scramble to fix their projects, neither of which were working properly still. Max Myers was literally turning red with frustration. I avoided making eye contact.

Olivia's experiment was two rows over. It was her attempt to prove the "three-second rule" was just a myth and not real science.

The three-second rule applies to those times when you drop something you're about to eat

on the floor. If you can pick it up within three seconds, it's supposed to be safe to eat. Olivia's display showed different types of mold growing on slices of whole wheat bread. It was gross. I think even Olivia would admit her experiment was a bit of a downer.

The school gym was crowded. Parents, students, and other adults I couldn't identify wandered up and down the aisles examining the different science experiments. It was thunderously loud and the atmosphere was surprisingly festive. My parents came by and took my picture, but I hadn't seen them since.

The judges—Principal Luntz; Mrs. Bird, our school nurse; and a guy named Edward G. Prentiss—were stopping at each display for a quick demonstration. Edward G. Prentiss had once been a student at Reed School and was now a big shot in business and science. Every year he volunteered to help pick our school's winner.

While the three judges strolled the aisles, I showed curious kids and parents how my electromagnet could pick up paper clips. I answered all their questions and was surprised at how easily I could discuss magnetism. I even explained to people how Earth was like a big magnet.

I was always careful to press only the first of my experiment's three buttons. I'd wait for the judges before I kicked it up a notch and hit the second button. Amp had told me to hit the third button only if I really needed it.

I did not plan on hitting the third button under any circumstances.

I was making sure my zipper was zipped when I was tapped on the shoulder. Judging time!

Mr. Prentiss looked first. He read all the paperwork I had mounted on the trifold cardboard standing up behind my electromagnet. He seemed to get more curious as he read. Out of the corner of my eye, I saw him nod a few times.

I waited and smiled uncomfortably as Mrs. Bird urgently scribbled notes on a clipboard. Principal Luntz seemed amazed the whole thing hadn't collapsed yet.

"Any relation to Taylor McGee?" Mr. Prentiss asked me.

"He's my little brother," I said. Mr. Prentiss

nodded, as if he already knew this and was just confirming it.

"Why choose iron for the core of your electromagnet?" Mr. Prentiss asked, turning suddenly to me, looking intently into my eyes. "Why not copper or steel or tin?"

"Well, all metals react differently to magnetic fields," I said. "Iron happens to be ideal, because it multiplies the magnetic field more than almost anything else. It can be hundreds or even thousands of times more powerful than most other metals. Iron was a no-brainer."

Mrs. Bird stared at me. Principal Luntz gasped. Mr. Prentiss chuckled, but in a good way. Nobody was more astonished than I was. How did I know this stuff?

"Let's see this beauty in action," Mr. Prentiss said, stepping aside to let me demonstrate.

With the first button, the paper clips skittered over to the electromagnet just as they had in the classroom.

I cleared my throat. "If I increase the current, it increases the power of the magnet." Finger trembling, I pushed the second button.

In the blink of an eye, my magnet ripped off Mr. Prentiss's fancy metal tie clip, Principal Luntz's glasses, and Mrs. Bird's clipboard. Even the metal box with the control switch for Davey Swope's spaghetti volcano was pulled from the next table and now stuck to the magnet, the cord to the volcano pulled tight.

Before I could turn it off, all the tacks holding my report on my trifold cardboard display ripped out of the wall and stuck to the magnet, making it look like a cactus. Papers were still fluttering every which way when I cut the magnet's power and everything was released.

"Wow," Mr. Prentiss said, plucking his tie clip out of the small pile of metal objects pulled to the magnet. He handed Principal Luntz's glasses back and returned Mrs. Bird's clipboard to her now-shaking hands. He looked me in the eyes and smiled. "You, young man, are certainly the one to beat."

I stared after them as they moved down to Davey Swope's smoldering volcano. I handed

Davey's volcano controller back to him with a helpless shrug, as if I wasn't sure why what just happened had just happened. But I hoped it was enough to get me an A.

Missing in Action

I sat alone at our kitchen table and stared at the blue ribbon.

First place.

I wasn't sure how to feel.

But I did know I didn't feel the way I should feel. Instead of proud, I felt uncomfortable. Uneasy. Worried. Nervous. I wasn't sure why.

It wasn't just beating Taylor, who had gotten the red second-place ribbon. It was something else. Of course, I wasn't sure how you're supposed to feel when an alien helps you win first place in your school's science fair. It had never happened to anyone in the history of mankind, so I was in all-new territory.

"Zack, I'll be ready to go in five minutes," Dad called from down the hallway. He was answering emails before he took me to the Tri-County

Science Fair Finals at our town's community center. The first-place winners from all twenty-nine elementary schools in three counties would be there.

Certainly I wouldn't win that. Or would I?

Just as I was beginning to accept the fact that I was my town's new science genius, I heard Amp's voice from under the kitchen table.

"It's over! It's truly over!" he screamed.

"Amp? What's wrong?" I said, sliding down under the table. "What's over?"

"We've got a major disaster on our hands," he said breathlessly.

"What?" I said. "We're almost out of the woods here. Stop worrying. Cheer up."

"What on earth are you talking about?" he shouted.

"What are *you* talking about?" I shouted back.

"What?" my dad called out from down the hall.

"Oh, nothing!" I called back. "Just talking to myself!"

"My spaceship has been stolen," Amp growled at me.

I laughed with relief. "Oh, Amp, it's not stolen, you goof. I moved it to my baseball bag—"

"I LOOKED IN THERE!" he whisper-screamed, grabbing me by the nose and yanking me down to his eye-level. "IT'S GONE!" he thundered in his squeaky voice.

I ran upstairs. The bag I kept my baseball equipment in was indeed unzipped and empty. I frantically turned over every square inch of my room. Amp's spaceship was gone.

89

"Now I can never leave this floofy planet," Amp whispered, staring out my window into the darkening sky.

"Zack, Olivia is on the phone!" Dad hollered from the bottom of the stairs. "She says she needs to talk to you urgently."

Amp and I stared at each other. "Maybe Olivia has it?" I gulped.

"I'll get it in your room!" I hollered back. I picked up Amp and ran down the hall to my parents' room. I sat on the bed and picked up the phone on my mom's nightstand. "HANG UP, DAD, I'VE GOT IT!" I yelled.

I could hear a lot of rustling sounds on the other side of the phone. Then I heard the phone downstairs click loudly as it was hung up.

"Olivia?" I said, but she didn't say anything. "Tell me you have Amp's ship. Do you have it? Hello? Olivia, can you hear me?"

"Zack, I'm here at the Tri-County Finals with my grandpa," she said. "I'm using my grandpa's cell phone."

My mind raced. I was sure her grandpa was listening, so Olivia was trying to be extra careful about what she said.

"Is he listening to you?"

"Yes, it's really fun here."

This told me he was listening. "Olivia, did you take Amp's spaceship? It's not here. We won't be mad if you took it, we just need to know."

She didn't speak for a few seconds. "Zack, I just thought you and your friend would want to know that Taylor got a ride here from a friend. He borrowed your silver football. I saw him with it, but I lost him in the crowd. It's here and I don't know what he's doing with it. I can't find him. You should come, quick." The phone went dead.

Amp, who had been listening next to me, just stared at me, his whole face trembling.

"DAD," I yelled. "WE HAVE TO LEAVE RIGHT NOW!"

17

Panic Attack

The community center was a zoo.

There were little kids running everywhere. Camera crews from the local news stations were filming with shockingly bright lights. Photographers from the paper popped their flashes. The air was filled with a steady roar of parents bragging about how smart their kids were.

Olivia had met me at the curb, where my dad dropped me before driving off to find a parking space. We raced inside and I walked right into the chaos.

"We've got to find Taylor immediately," I said to Olivia, scanning my eyes over the noisy crowd moving through row after row of impressive-looking experiments.

I noticed that the kids demonstrating their

science projects were dressed up. The girls wore sharp, bright dresses. Many of the boys wore little V-neck sweaters with matching clip-on ties. I looked down at my muddy sneakers, jeans, and old hoodie sweatshirt.

"You look like a science genius who's down on his luck," Olivia said.

"I couldn't find my tie," I said with a shrug.

"Did you bring Amp?" Olivia asked.

"He's in my pocket," I said. "He has this invisibility trick, but he explained in the car it doesn't work on this many brains at once."

"I have no idea what that even means," she said.

"ZACK MCGEE!"

It was Mrs. Bird. She looked upset. She grabbed me by the arm with her bony fingers. "They're waiting, let's go! If you're not there in less than a minute, you'll be disqualified!"

"Yeah, about that," I said. "I'm kind of busy right now."

With that, she took me by the ear and began pulling me away—which I'm pretty sure you're not allowed to do even if you are the school nurse. But no one seemed to want to intervene.

"Find Taylor!" I called back to Olivia. "I'll meet you in a minute."

Thankfully, as Mrs. Bird shoved me in front of the waiting judges, I noticed my project had been set up for me, fully intact and bolted to a desk that was bolted to the floor. Amp's precious gizmo remained in its place near the third button.

To be honest, I can't even remember what I said to the panel of judges waiting for me at my science project. Mr. Prentiss was one of the judges, but there were now four other judges I did not recognize. Some of them asked me questions. I wasn't sure if Amp was sending me information from my pocket with his alien hocus-pocus, but I was impressed with my answers even as I said them.

The magnet worked as it had earlier in the day, pulling the tacks from my display and sending papers fluttering everywhere. That had a big impact. The judges lost a pen, a necklace, and an oversized State of Texas belt buckle to my magnet.

There was lots of nodding and soaring eyebrows, so I know it went pretty well, even if I couldn't tell you a single thing they said.

As the judges walked off to the next experiment, I also started to run off, but first I spotted Max Myers in the crowd. He had watched my demonstration. "Max! Max!" I called, waving him over. "Could you do me a favor? Could you keep an eye on my experiment for a minute? If anyone touches it or starts pushing those buttons, head-butt them."

"Uh, okay. But I don't think my mom will like me head-butting anybody," he said with a troubled look on his face. Then he softened. "Don't worry, McGee. I'll stand guard for you. We're teammates now, right?"

"Teammates?"

"Didn't you see? They posted the cuts online. You're on my baseball team now. We're both Badgers, buddy."

"Whoa," I said. "I didn't know that. Thanks!"

With that, I ran off, feeling bad about not being able to feel good about making the travel baseball team.

Navigating the science fair was like running through a field of corn. I couldn't see anything over the heads of all the adults, and I certainly saw no sign of Olivia or Taylor. I ran past my mom once and she said, "Jeepers, Zack!" as I ran by.

"What's taking so long?" Amp shouted through my pocket.

"I'm trying!" I yelped. "I can't find Taylor anywhere."

Just as I was about to exit through a side door to see if I could find anybody outside, somebody yanked on the hood of my sweatshirt and spun me around.

Olivia.

"Look!" she said, pointing to the left of the stage at the end of the room. There I saw Taylor wearing a swollen green backpack. He was opening a door that led to the backstage area. He was being followed by a puzzled and slightly annoyed looking Mr. Prentiss. Taylor waved him into the doorway. "He's going to show the spaceship to that judge guy with the fancy suit!" Olivia exclaimed.

"GET MY SHIP!" Amp roared in my head.

And with that, Olivia and I tore off to rescue the spaceship with no plan other than an ace in the hole—or at least an alien in the pocket.

Showdown

"**H**and it over, thief!" I demanded when I threw the stage door open.

"What is this thing?" Taylor said, lifting Amp's gleaming spaceship out of the backpack. He held it up for Mr. Prentiss to see.

"My little brother stole that from my room," I told Mr. Prentiss, who seemed at a complete loss for what to do.

We were all cramped together in a tiny space at the bottom of some dark stairs that led backstage. Taylor was close enough to try tackling him, but I didn't want to accidentally damage Amp's ship.

"Zack's been hiding this in his room, and it's no hamster cage," Taylor said, lifting the spaceship like he was going to throw it down. "Just look at this thing, Mr. Prentiss! You might be able

to figure out what it is."

So that was his plan: he wanted to see if Mr. Prentiss could identify it.

"Take it easy with that, Taylor," Olivia warned.

"Hey, I don't want to get mixed up with any family squabbles," Mr. Prentiss said uncomfortably. "I'm needed onstage. I don't have time for—"

"You stole it, Taylor," I yelled, my voice cracking with emotion.

Taylor tried to ignore us. He stepped toward Mr. Prentiss. "Feel how light it is. It's not even metal. I don't know what it's made out of. Just hold it!"

Mr. Prentiss reached out for it, seemingly mesmerized by curiosity.

"Oh, forget this," I heard Amp say inside my head.

Suddenly, Mr. Prentiss straightened up like he'd just stepped in something. His eyes grew wide and then he started to gag. "I smell . . . horse poop."

"What?" Olivia said, stunned.

"Amp," I groaned. He was using his Erdian mind trick to cause Mr. Prentiss to experience the scent of poop.

"It's terrible!" Mr. Prentiss cried, quickly looking at the bottoms of his expensive shoes.

"Horse poop?" Taylor exclaimed. "I don't smell anything."

I could hear announcements outside in the main hall. The crowd cheered and clapped.

Amp was trying to force Mr. Prentiss out of this tiny space. Amp could make a person think of practically anything for a short period of time.

And the sense of smell, Amp once told me, was the easiest to mess with.

"Oh, it's terrible," Mr. Prentiss said, swatting at the air in front of him. "And now it's mixed with cafeteria food," he gagged. "It's like it was just burrito day in here."

Taylor screwed up his face and stared at the spaceship. "Poop? Burritos? Maybe this thing makes you crazy!"

"I have to get out of here," Mr. Prentiss cried. He turned and crashed through the door, letting in another round of cheering from the crowd. The door swung closed, leaving us in the dim light again.

"Agh, I thought he'd never leave," Amp said, emerging from my pocket and climbing up the sleeve of my sweatshirt.

"WHAT IS THAT?!?" Taylor croaked. He let go of the spaceship and it dropped toward the floor. Olivia was fast enough to snatch it out of the air just before it hit the ground.

"Amp," I stammered. "You didn't make yourself invisible!"

"Oh, right, I forgot," he said casually, looking

103

over at Taylor. "Hey, I can't think straight in that pocket. Not enough air, I guess."

"Your doll . . . it's alive," Taylor said in a soft, quivering voice.

"Now look at what you've done," I said to Amp, plucking him off my shoulder. "Now my brother knows about you, and he's impossible to shut up."

The crowd outside erupted in laughter, then cheered and clapped again.

Olivia stuffed the spaceship back in the backpack. "We need to get out of here."

The crowd cheered again, as if they were responding to each of the things we said.

"I'll have to erase some of his short-term memory," Amp said, looking at me.

I stared at him for a second and then said, "Fine! Just do it quickly."

"Wait! What?" Taylor said, panicked.

Amp stared at Taylor and squinted.

A second later, Taylor got a blank look on his face. He blinked. His body relaxed. The fear melted away. "Where am I?" he asked, looking around. "Oh my gosh, what is that—that creature you're holding?!" he asked, clearly horrified.

"AMP, YOU DID IT AGAIN! YOU FORGOT TO MAKE YOURSELF INVISIBLE!"

Olivia moaned. "You guys are killing me."

"Oh dear, that was my mistake," Amp said. "Totally my fault."

"Well, it certainly wasn't *my* fault," I snapped.

"That doll is alive!" Taylor gasped again, stepping back toward the stairs.

As if on cue, the crowd erupted with laughter outside the door.

"Hold on, Taylor, he'll erase your memory again in a second."

And for the second time in two minutes, Amp erased Taylor's short-term memory, but this time Amp remembered to make himself invisible to Taylor.

"Where am I?" Taylor asked, looking around again. "Why is Olivia wearing my backpack?"

Olivia pulled Taylor up gently by the shoulder. "C'mon, let's go, Taylor."

I slipped Amp back in my pocket and followed Olivia and Taylor out the door.

Four hundred eyeballs zeroed in on my entrance and I froze.

"OH, THERE HE IS! THERE'S OUR THIRD FINALIST! AND JUST IN TIME! LET'S HEAR IT FOR ZACK MCGEE, EVERYBODY!"

The crowd in front of me erupted in applause, hoots, and whistles.

And I thought this night couldn't get any weirder. Boy, was I wrong.

Meltdown

I shuffled out onto the stage, surprised by the volume of the crowd's welcome. My town really does love science geeks.

The two other better-dressed finalists looked at me with cold stares. I could see my parents in the front of the crowd. Mom was fanning her flushed face. Dad was holding up his smartphone, shooting video.

I spied Olivia on the far right of the crowd. Taylor stood next to her, blinking in confusion. Olivia nodded at me. I forgot to nod back.

A short, round man with a scrawny mustache and thick glasses introduced me and my experiment with his microphone. The crowd clapped again politely. I figured I had missed the first two demonstrations, which explained the rude stares from the other two finalists.

Mustache guy guided me over to my experiment, which was set up at stage right. I wondered if Max Myers had head-butted anybody.

Just past the table with my electromagnet were the judges, who all stood in a cluster and smiled at me politely.

Mr. Mustache began to ask me simple questions, but I was having trouble concentrating. My mouth was dry and my tongue felt like a day-old bologna sandwich. I wasn't a big fan of speaking in front of my class, and this was my first time in front of several hundred people. I accidentally said "maggot" instead of "magnet," and the crowd tittered and stirred uncomfortably.

"Hold it together, Zack," Amp said inside my head.

Mustache Man fixed his stare on me. "What is the most important thing you learned in building your experiment?"

Nobody had asked me that question. I wasn't ready for it. A hanging curveball when I was waiting for a slider.

"Well," I said, a little too close to the microphone, and the speakers on the stage erupted in screeching feedback. I stepped back and smiled. Deep breath. Just like I'd do if I were facing a tough pitcher. *Focus, Zack, before getting back in the batter's box.* "Well," I said again in a softer voice. This time there was no screeching. "I learned not to lean in too close to a microphone."

The crowd laughed, and for a moment, I thought I really did have a chance to win this thing. "Actually, the thing I learned is the importance of good friends. Two of my good friends encouraged me to finish this project. I couldn't have done it without them."

"AAAAAAW," the crowd said with a collective sigh, clearly finding my response adorable.

I saw a look of confusion come over my mom's face. "Two?" she mouthed silently to my dad, holding up two fingers. Dad didn't notice. His eyes were glued to the video image recording on his phone.

From there, I proceeded to demonstrate my experiment.

As always, when I hit the second button the tacks flew out of my trifold cardboard and strange metal objects skittered across the room. Mr. Mustache's microphone was yanked from his hand and the crowd laughed. He pulled on it, but it wasn't going to come free. I stepped in front of the experiment and hit the second button again, releasing all the metal objects.

Mustache Man stumbled away to the far side of the stage with his microphone and said something clever, and the crowd laughed and clapped in approval. "Now, I see there's a third button on here. I know the judges have been curious about what it does."

I could feel my stomach drop like I was on roller coaster that had just done a three-sixty, upside down, at top speed. "Oh, that . . . ," I said, inadvertently stepping back.

"Do you mind?" he said, smiling and leaning over to push it. "Gentleman, I'd suggest you hold on to your money clips." I think he thought he was being funny.

I could feel Amp telepathically telling me not to let him do it, but I guess with all the bright lights and people staring, I just got stuck. The best I could do was let out a half-swallowed, "No . . ." as he pushed the button.

For a moment, nothing happened. Mr. Mustache straightened up, confused. But then the lights dimmed. The stage speakers shot sparks. The microphone once again flew past me and collided with the magnet with a *CLANG!*

In an instant, the desks with the other experiments started sliding toward the stage from all corners of the community center. The lights in the ceiling exploded, one after another, from the one right above us to the ones all the way in the back. The crowd was pitched into complete darkness. The

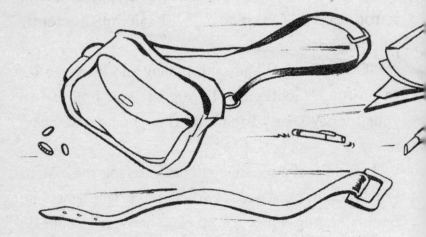

curtains behind me were pulled down, their tiny rings sticking to the growing ball of metal objects that had been pulled onto the magnet. If anything, it seemed to be gaining in power. Random objects were whizzing dangerously past me toward the magnet. One lady with a really big ring on was being pulled toward it. Another guy wearing a big American flag pin was also being dragged up on stage. On direct order from

Amp, I hit the floor and covered my head.

Then, to everyone's terror, the ceiling started to groan and make loud cracking noises. Without looking up, I somehow knew that the giant heating and air conditioning unit on the roof of the building was being pulled down to my magnet.

I scrambled over the debris and reached for the third button. My only hope was to turn it off. But it was now covered by a collection of metal objects. There was a small opening. Too small for my hand to fit through—but not, I quickly realized, for Amp. "I need your help, buddy."

And like any good soldier, Amp scrambled out of my pocket to help, not even pausing to consider his own safety. He ran up my arm and jumped head-first into the opening a moment before a stapler flew out of nowhere and closed the hole. I heard a scream and turned to see a loose metal pipe flying straight toward me. This was it. My life flashed before my eyes. I was a goner.

But then, there was a high-pitched "Got it," followed by a click, and all the metal objects stuck to the magnet collapsed to the floor. The pipe stopped

in midflight, inches from my face, and dropped to the floor with a thud.

I exhaled.

A moment later I was helped to my feet by Mr. Prentiss.

"I don't know what happened," I said as innocently as I could.

"Science is like that sometimes," he said. "But the rule should always be 'Safety first.' That's the lesson you should learn here tonight." He gently patted me on the shoulder.

"Sorry," I said.

"Well, that really was something," he said, looking over his shoulder at my innocent-looking bolt-magnet. "We should talk more, Mr. McGee." And with that, he left the stage as my parents scurried up to make sure that I was okay.

"Hey, does that mean we won?" Amp asked in my head. He had somehow snuck back into the safety of the front pocket of my sweatshirt.

"I doubt that," I said. "I think not going to jail will be viewed as the big victory here tonight."

Keeping It Secret

Before arriving at the breakfast table the next morning, I snuck down the stairs and returned the bare bolt to the award plaque in my dad's office.

I stepped back and looked at the bolt. It was now charred with black stuff and the middle was sort of droopy and twisted from overheating. It looked terrible, but at least it was back.

I sighed.

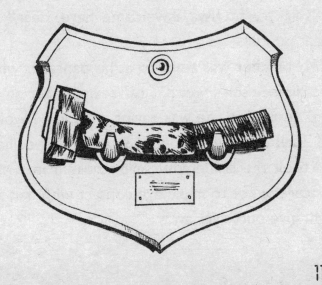

117

After Mr. Prentiss had walked away from me on the stage last night, Amp and I had quickly pulled off the secret parts he had taken out of his spaceship and hid them in my socks.

When the lights came back on and the judges closely examined my project, they couldn't figure out what had happened. They were all puzzled. But Mr. Prentiss kept giving me a knowing smile. He knew I was keeping secrets.

In the kitchen, I saw Olivia was once again eating breakfast at my house. We'd have to start charging her rent.

She saw me looking at her. "My grandpa went fishing early this morning," she said as she poured herself a glass of juice. "So sue me."

"Oh, you're always welcome here, dear," Mom said.

My brother was stabbing at his pancakes with his electric fork. "It's weird, I can't remember anything from yesterday," he was saying. "It's like I woke up and Zack was walking onto the stage at the finals."

I took the last empty seat across from Olivia. I was careful not to make eye contact with her, as we might give ourselves away.

My parents exchanged a look and Mom patted Taylor's shoulder. "I've already called Dr. Bell, sweetie. You have an appointment this afternoon. I'm sure he'll just want to run some tests. His nurse said you probably shouldn't go to school today."

"What?" Taylor said. "I'm going to school! Everybody will be talking about how Zack destroyed the finals. My friend Jimmy said the cops might come and arrest Zack."

"That's just silly," Mom said, fanning herself with her napkin. "It's not Zack's fault that his experiment worked better than he could have expected."

I looked over at the yellow ribbon that was now held to the refrigerator with a big pineapple-shaped magnet. Third place. Not bad, I guess. I was actually just relieved nobody had gotten hurt. I had received a check for fifty dollars, plus a free subscription to *Kid Science* magazine—and an A, which meant I could play ball this season. And even though that was all I really cared about to begin with, I did have to admit that building a superpowered electromagnet was a lot cooler than I thought.

I hadn't spoken to Amp since we left the community center last night. I was giving him the silent treatment—and he was doing the same to me. I think he felt bad about what had happened.

"Oh, Zack, that nice Mr. Prentiss called and left you a message," Mom said.

"He did?" I said.

"He did?" Olivia said.

"He did?" Taylor said, and burped loudly.

Mom and Olivia laughed. See? They were just encouraging this behavior.

"What did he say?" Dad asked, looking at Taylor with his unhappy face.

"Something about you coming to one of his businesses for a grand tour," Mom said. "Maybe having a summer job set aside for you," she added, smiling at me with pride. "Despite last night, he sees promise in you."

"Yeah, the promise of more destruction," Taylor said glumly, stabbing at his pancake. "Did he say anything about me?"

"Oh, I'm sorry, honey," Mom said, patting his shoulder again. "He just mentioned Zack."

"There are some things I may need Mr. Prentiss's help with," I said, shooting a look at Olivia.

"Oh, and Coach Lopez left a message, too," Dad

said, looking at me with pride. "Looks like the Badgers have Zack McGee on the roster as their new catcher."

"Backup catcher, Dad," Taylor corrected. "Backup catcher."

"Yep, I heard about that," I said. "I'm in the big leagues now."

Mom got up, came around the table, and gave me a squeeze. Then she messed up my hair. "Things are getting more interesting for you, Zackary Frederick McGee."

"Oh, that is an understatement," Olivia said.

As we hustled out the door to catch the bus to school, Amp finally broke his silence.

"Okay, I'm sorry, Zack," Amp said, inside my head. "I've learned my lesson. From now on, I'll be a perfect little alien."

"Oh? We'll see about that, Amp," I responded inside my head. I looked up at my bedroom window as Olivia and I jogged across the front lawn. I couldn't see him from this distance, but I was pretty sure he was watching me from my windowsill.

Little did I know he was hiding in the front pocket of my backpack.

Try It Yourself: Building Your Own Electromagnet

Electromagnets use a flow of electricity, called electric current, to produce magnetic fields. You're probably already familiar with magnetic fields since you can feel their effects, such as the pulling force a permanent magnet makes toward a ferromagnetic material—like the door of your refrigerator. Electromagnets are cool because you can vary how strong they are by making simple changes to their construction.

YOU WILL NEED: a pencil-shaped piece of metal that a magnet can grab (like a bolt from the garage), insulated wire (the kind called "magnet wire" is the very best), a battery, and something to grab (like a handful of paper clips), and an adult to supervise.

Magnet Construction

1. Take the pencil-shaped piece of metal and start wrapping the insulated wire around it. Wind carefully to fit in lots of wraps. Leave about a 6" tail of wire sticking off each end so you can attach the leads to a battery.

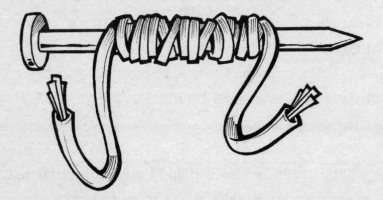

2. Make sure the ends of the wire are stripped so you can attach the metal core to the battery. If you're using wire with plastic insulation on it, you will need the help of a parent to use a knife or wire strippers to expose the copper underneath. If you found some magnet wire, use sandpaper to remove the lacquer on the outside of the copper wire. It can be hard to see since it's clear.

3. Connect the wire ends to your battery. Voila! You should be able to attract a number of paper clips to the end of the metal piece, which is the electromagnet's core. Congratulations—you have built an electromagnet! You might not know it, but you're surrounded by electromagnets very similar to the one you just built. The closest ones might be inside the speakers of your TV or cell phone.

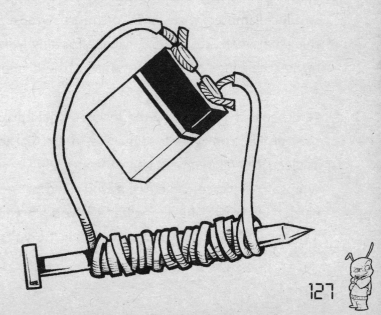

Experiment Time

1. What would it take to supercharge your electromagnet like Amp did for Zack? In the book, Amp intensifies Zack's electromagnet strength by concentrating extra magnetic fields through the magnet's core, which increased its grabbing power. You can do the same by intensifying the magnetic field going through the core of your own electromagnet. Do this by adding more wraps of wire onto your electromagnet. The more wraps you add, the more power the electric current can add to the magnetic field. The more power in the magnetic field you have, the stronger your magnet! How many wraps do you need to pick up twice as many paper clips as before? Try using a smaller-diameter wire to fit on more wraps, something between 20 and 28 gauge. For any wire, the higher the gauge number, the smaller the diameter.

2. Another way to intensify the magnetic field produced by your electromagnet is to increase the actual amount of electricity (aka *current*) going through all of your wire wraps. To increase the current, you need to "push" it harder by using a higher voltage. If you started with a normal AA battery, you were putting 1.5 volts onto

the wire. You can push the electricity twice as hard by adding another battery in the series, giving the electricity 3 volts of pushing. By pushing twice as hard, you'll get double the current, which should roughly double the strength of your electromagnet!

3. In the book, Amp "guides" extra magnetic fields into Zack's electromagnet core. You can also guide the magnetic field produced by your electromagnet. Magnetic fields like to flow through some materials quite a bit, and other materials not so much. Air is not a magnetic field's favorite substance to flow through, especially compared to a ferromagnetic material like iron or steel. Find another pencil-shaped piece of iron or steel, like a bolt or a nail, and hold it at the end of your electromagnet while it's turned on. What happens at the end of the nail? It acts like a magnet itself, because you're using it to guide the magnetic field. Just like Amp does.

Notes About Safety

- Down at low voltages, electromagnets are pretty safe. But naturally, you're going to want to add more batteries to make your electromagnet more powerful. This is awesome, and you should do it. But be careful! When experimenting with more powerful batteries like 9-volts and beyond, make sure to have an adult supervising. And wear safety glasses in case you get a spark.

- You'll probably notice that when you run your electromagnet for a while, it gets hot. This is because most of the electricity from the battery is dissipated as heat by going through the electrical resistance of your wire. If you use bigger batteries, it's going to get hot faster. If you use really big batteries, you could burn yourself or even melt the insulation or the wire. Use caution and always start small.

Troubleshooting

- If your electromagnet doesn't seem to work, the usual culprits are either a dead battery, too small of a battery, or the most common problem: not making a connection between the wire and the battery in the first place. Ensure you have a good contact directly with the copper in your wire by carefully restripping the plastic insulation off the wire. If you used magnet wire, spend a little extra time sanding the insulative lacquer off the conductor to ensure a good contact.

Read a sneak peek of book three
of the Alien in My Pocket series:

Radio Active

"It smells like the devil burped in here."

Olivia had just shut the door of my room. She pulled two rolls of SweeTarts out of her pocket and tossed them to Amp, who was still sitting on my alarm clock.

"It smells like that because he keeps eating those fart pills," I said, still hunched over my math homework. "Hey, did you get the one about the train leaving San Francisco at eight p.m.?" I asked, turning around in my chair.

Olivia is in my class at Reed School. Schoolwork isn't difficult for her. Olivia just sort of knows stuff. She usually finishes her math homework while everyone else is packing up to leave for the day. She'd be a real brain if she weren't so weird and didn't talk so much.

"Forty-eight miles an hour is the answer," she said, watching Amp flip SweeTarts into his mouth.

"Forty-eight?" I croaked. "I have five hundred forty-four!"

"How is that possible?" She laughed, shaking her head at me. "What train travels that fast, Whacky Zacky?"

"Maybe those Japanese bullet trains. I saw them on TV."

"They don't go that fast," she corrected me. "Two hundred miles an hour, tops."

"We have trainlike vehicles back on Erde," Amp said, once again bragging about how great things were on his planet. "They travel about as fast as sound travels here."

"I've told you before about talking with your mouth full," I grumbled, turning back to my incorrect math problem. "You may have fast trains on Erde, but we have something called manners here on this planet."

"Has he been this grumpy the whole time?" Olivia asked Amp.

"Since he got home. Surprisingly, math makes him angry."

Honestly, all our meetings about fixing Amp's busted spaceship, getting him off this planet, and returning my life to normal went like this. What was the point of meeting if we never accomplished anything except pointing out all the things I do wrong? I was so not the problem.

There was a knock on my bedroom door. Olivia quickly moved to block the view of Amp from the doorway.

She always did this, even though Amp could easily make himself invisible to someone. He uses one of his Jedi mind tricks. He basically erases your memory of seeing him as you see him, so you instantly forget you're seeing him while you're looking at him.

I know, it sounds complicated. You get used to it. But Olivia always forgets he can do that.

The door clicked open and my little brother poked his head in.

"I heard you have SweeTarts," he said. "I want some."

"Go away, Taylor," I groaned from my desk. "We're busy."

Olivia reached into her pocket and tossed Taylor a roll of SweeTarts. He intentionally missed the catch so he could step all the way into my

3

room. "Hey, what are you guys doing?" he asked, looking around. "It smells like burning toothpaste in here."

Taylor knew something was up. He knew I was hiding a secret, and he'd dedicated his life to figuring out what it was. He'd even built an army of spy robots to help him. Fortunately, I'd destroyed most of them when I caught them in my room.

My parents are convinced Taylor is some kind of genius. He *is* only in the first grade and building robots. But I don't care. I think he's only a genius at annoying me.

I got up and pushed him out of my room. "Go play with your robots, you Nosy Nelly." I closed the door on him and leaned my back against it.

"But I want to hang out with you guys," he said from the other side of the door.

"Buzz off!" I shouted. I heard him walk down the squeaky hallway.

Olivia sat up on my bed. She had an odd look on her face. It was almost white, like she'd seen a ghost.

"What's wrong with you?" I ask. "Is Amp's gas cloud getting to you?"

"How did he know I had SweeTarts? I didn't tell him, and you didn't tell him, so how did he know?"

The three of us stared at each other.

Without looking down, Olivia unclipped the walkie-talkie from her pocket. She held it up and stared at it. "That little sneak is listening in on our walkie-talkie conversations."

"What a clever idea," Amp whispered.

I looked at them both. I was pretty sure steam was coming out of my ears. "A clever idea that the little worm is gonna pay for."